HEY, KID!

HEY, KID!

By Rita Golden Gelman

Illustrated by Carol Nicklaus

A Snuggle & Read Story Book

AN AVON CAMELOT BOOK

AVON BOOKS
A division of
The Hearst Corporation
959 Eighth Avenue
New York, New York 10019

First Camelot Printing, October, 1978
Second Printing

AVON TRADEMARK REG. U.S. PAT. OFF. AND IN
OTHER COUNTRIES, MARCA REGISTRADA, HECHO EN
U.S.A.

Printed in the U.S.A.

10 9 8 7 6 5 4 3

FOR JAN

"Hey, Kid!"
"Who, me?"

"I have this thing.
It's white and black and gray.
I'm gonna let you have it, Kid.
Today's your lucky day."

He cut the rope.

Unlocked the locks.

He pulled the nails out.

He banged the box until it cracked.

And then I heard a shout.

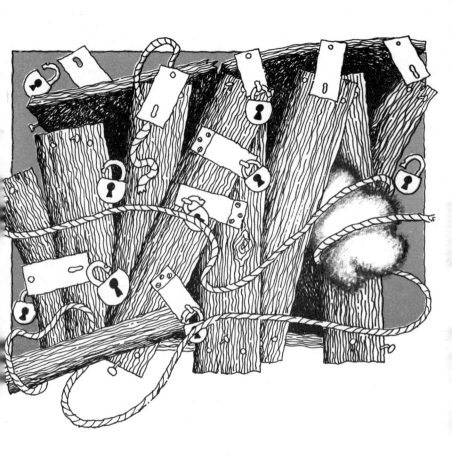

"I'm free. I'm free," said something.
"I'm free. Now let me out!"

The box began to open.

The wood began to tear.

And then I saw the nicest thing.

"Hello," he said.

"I'm here."

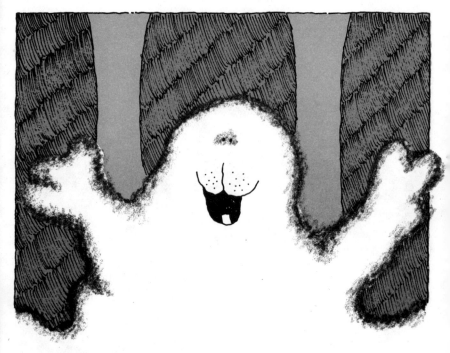

"Take me.

Take me in your house.

Show me where I sleep.

Show me where the TV is.

I'm yours," he said.

"To keep."

"Hey, Boy," I called.

"I love my thing.

Thank you.

Won't you stay?"

But that boy,

he never heard me.

He was miles and miles away.

"Come on," said Sam.

"Let's go. Let's sing.

I want to sing a song."

And then he started singing it.
He sang it all day long.

He sang it during dinner.
He sang it just for me.
And he sang that song the
whole time I was watching my TV.

Then he stopped and started talking.
And I had to be polite.
So I listened to his talking.
And he talked right through the night.

He talked about a man who had
a donkey on his head.
And he talked about a cow who ate
her chicken soup in bed.

At three o'clock he talked about
a princess and some cheese.

And at six o'clock he talked about
a mouse who couldn't sneeze.

At breakfast time he talked
about a noisy, yellow hawk.

I said, "Excuse me, Sam.
I think I'll take a little walk."

"I'll come," said Sam.

"I love to walk.

I love to sing.

I love to talk.

I'll come with you

and sing my song."

"Oh, no," I thought.

"That song's too long."

He sang his song at lunchtime, too.
He sang it in the bath.

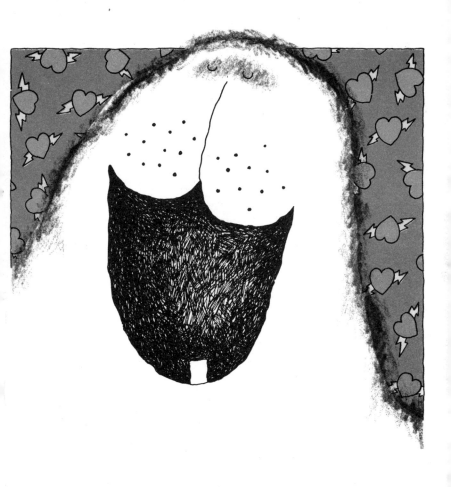

He sang it after dinner
while I tried to do my math.

Then I ran up to the attic,
And I shut and locked the door.
And I said, "You better cut it out.
Don't sing that any more."

"Okay," he said.
"I'll talk instead."
He talked right through the hole.

He talked about a car with wings.
He talked about a mole.

"Don't talk," I said.
"You've talked enough.
There's nothing more to say."

"Oh, no," he said.
"You're very wrong.
Why I could talk all day."

And while I got a big, strong box,
he talked about some snails.

And then he had to tell me
how a walrus cuts its nails.

And when I got the 20 locks,
he talked about the snow.

And as I banged the cover shut,
he talked about a crow.

And then I took my wagon.

And I walked across the town.

I walked for miles and miles and miles.

Up the hills and down.

I found a place far, far away.
And then I stopped to look.

I saw a kid outside his house,
looking at a book.

"Hey, Kid!" I said.
"I have this thing.
  It's white and black and gray.
  I'm gonna let you have it, Kid.
  Today's your lucky day."